The Frog Who Would Be King

by Kate Walker

illustrated by David Cox

THERE WAS ONCE A FROG WHO dreamed of being someone special, someone brave and noble. He wanted to be a king, but he knew that such a thing could never happen to him while he lived in a lily pond. So he ventured forth into the world to find a princess. For, like all frogs, he had heard the story of the princess whose kiss of love had changed a frog into a handsome prince.

It was a dewy morning when he finally hopped up to a castle and stationed himself on a princess's balcony. Feeling rather nervous, he took a deep breath and croaked, "Knee-deep, knee-deep."

The princess came rushing from her chamber, and it was love at first sight for both of them. The frog had never seen anyone so beautiful. Even though he was only a little frog and she was a tall princess, he thought her the loveliest, daintiest creature he had ever seen.

Her name was Lil and she thought this
frog was the most perfect in all the world
— so sweet and shiny and green.
She gave him the noblest name she could
think of — Reginald. Their romance
blossomed like a well-watered buttercup,
and finally Reginald decided to propose.

"Dear Lil," he began, holding her little
finger with his sucker pad, "could you
possibly overlook my frogginess and
be my wife?"

Lil swooned with emotion and fainted on the spot. Reginald hopped back and forth from the goldfish pond with water to splash on her face: back and forth, back and forth, trying to wake her up so she could give her answer.

His efforts were rewarded. Her answer was "yes." She would marry him, frog or not.

"Marry a frog?" her father roared when she told him. "You can't be serious. Don't you know that the man you marry will one day become king in my place?"

"Yes, Father," she said, "I know, and I think Reginald would make a wonderful king. He's wise and courageous and kind."

"I don't care if his blankets are made from boy scout badges," cried the king. "He's still a frog, and he's not going to sit on my throne!"

Lil came away broken-hearted, for she must have been the only person in the world who had not heard the story of the frog and the princess. Reginald soon told her.

"You see, my dear," he said, "one kiss is all it takes. I'll turn into a prince and our problems will be over. So, pucker up."

"But Reginald," she said, "you'll give me warts!"

"Lil dear, toads, not frogs, give you warts."

"Sorry dearest." She raised him to her lips, closed her eyes, and . . .

Smooooooch!

"Oh, no!" she cried, "You're still a frog!"

He looked glumly at his greenness.
"I can't understand it. Our ingredients are right. I'm a frog, you're a princess, and we love each other enough to turn a dozen tadpoles into a ready-made family."

"I'll marry you anyway," said Lil.
"I wouldn't care if you were an ugly old toad."

But Reginald did care. It was his
dream to become king. He had come a
long way from the lily pond, and he was
not going to turn back now.

"I'll go and see the local witch,"
he said. "She should be able to tell us
what's gone wrong."

"And I'll have a chat with the court
magician," said Lil, "and see
what he says."

So Reginald told the witch what had happened, or rather what had *not* happened. She nodded her head and said, "Frog, whoever told you that story got it mixed up. That wasn't a frog that the princess kissed and turned into a prince. It was a toad. Why, anyone can change a toad with a little smack on the lips. But frogs are different. You can kiss frogs till the cows come home and they'll still be frogs."

Reginald turned away dragging his flippers in despair.

"Of course," said the witch, "what we could do is turn you into a toad first, and *then* into a prince."

Reginald came bouncing back.
"Could you really do that?"

"Sure could," she said, giving a
toothless smile. "In fact, it's a long time
since I've kissed a handsome prince."

Slowly the witch brewed the murky
potion. Reginald tried to hurry her, but
she would not be rushed.

"These are one-way spells," she
warned him, "and we wouldn't want
any mistakes to be made because there's
no coming back for seconds."

When the potion was ready, Reginald took one sip from the spoon and immediately puffed up into a big, brown toad. The witch bent down to him.

"All right, sweetie," she said, "give us a kiss and let's see how handsome you are."

"I'm terribly sorry, Madame," replied Reginald, "but I am engaged to Lil, and it wouldn't be right for me to kiss another."

Reginald bounded back to the castle for the kiss of love that would turn him into a prince at last. His lily pad dreams were about to come true.

When Reginald came to the princess's chamber, the court magician opened the door. Being very tall, he looked down on Reginald from a great height.

"What have we here?" he said.

"I'm Reginald, the princess's frog," he answered, "only I had the witch turn me into a toad."

"And I must say, she's done a fine job too," said the magician, picking Reginald up to examine his warts. "Yes, very fine work. Almost as good as my *own* efforts, wouldn't you agree?"

Saying that, he placed Reginald on a lotus leaf in the goldfish pond, right next to a little green frog.

"Oh Reginald," the frog cried in a sweet voice, "all our problems are solved. We're not different anymore." The frog was Lil.

"But we *are*," he croaked. "You're a beautiful frog and I'm an ugly old toad."

"I don't care," she said. And she put her little sucker foot on his big warty flipper and gave him a kiss.

In an instant, a handsome young man appeared in the water beside her.

"Oh Lil!"

"Oh Reginald!"

Lil's kiss had changed Reginald into a tall and dashing prince, but she was still a green and shiny frog. However, after the initial shock, they both decided that it didn't matter if one of them was a frog. Nothing had really changed. Their love was the same. They had just swapped places, that was all.

The king changed his mind, though.
He was only too happy to have Reginald
marry his daughter now. Who else would,
now that she was a frog?

So Reginald married his princess, and in
time became king, while all the other frogs
still sat on their lily pads catching tasteless
flies and not daring to dream of all the
greater things they could be.

Published in the United States of America in 1995 by

MONDO Publishing

By arrangement with MULTIMEDIA INTERNATIONAL (UK) LTD

For information contact:
Mondo Publishing
980 Avenue of Americas
New York, NY 10018

MONDO is a registered trademark of Mondo Publishing

Visit our web site at http://www.mondopub.com

Cover redesign by MM Design 2000
Printed in the United States of America
First Mondo printing, April 1995
02 03 04 05 06   9 8 7 6 5 4 3

Originally published in Australia in 1987 by Horwitz Publications Pty Ltd
Original development by Snowball Educational

Library of Congress Cataloging-in-Publication Data
Walker, Kate.
    The frog who would be king / by Kate Walker ; illustrated by David Cox.
        p.   cm.
    Summary: Reginald and Lil's love fore each other is complicated by the
fact that he is a frog and she is a princess.
    ISBN 1-57255-020-1 (pb) — ISBN 1-57255-021-X (big bk.)
    [1. Frogs—Fiction. 2. Princesses—Fiction.] I. Cox, David, 1933- ill.
II. Title.
PZ7.W15298Fr   1995
[E]—dc20
                                                                95-5429
                                                                CIP
                                                                AC